MY FIRST STORY 2017

Welcome!

Dear Reader,

Welcome to a world of imagination!

My First Story was designed for 5-7 year-olds as an introduction to creative writing and to promote an enjoyment of reading and writing from an early age.

The simple, fun storyboards give even the youngest and most reluctant writers the chance to become interested in literacy by giving them a framework within which to shape their ideas. Pupils could also choose to write without the storyboards, allowing older children to let their creativity flow as much as possible, encouraging the use of imagination and descriptive language.

We believe that seeing their work in print will inspire a love of reading and writing and give these young writers the confidence to develop their skills in the future.

There is nothing like the imagination of children, and this is reflected in the creativity and individuality of the stories in this anthology. I hope you'll enjoy reading their first stories as much as we have.

Jenni Harrison

Editorial Manager

Imagine...

Each child was given the beginning of a story and then chose one of five storyboards, using the pictures and their imagination to complete the tale. You can view the storyboards at the end of this book.

There was also the option to create their own story using a blank template.

The beginning...

One sunny day, Emma and Ben were walking the dog.

Suddenly, the dog started barking at a magic door hidden in a tree.

They opened the door and it took them to...

... what is on the other side of the door? Tell us your story!

SOUTH WEST TALES
CONTENTS

Winner:

Olivier Kalinowski (6) -   1
Blackhorse Primary School,
Bristol

Bickleigh Down CE Primary School, Plymouth

Rihanna Andrews (7)	2
Isabel Joshy (6)	3
Sienna Martin (6)	4
Lilia Kilpatrick (7)	5
Isla Stringer (6)	6
Troy Johnson (7)	7
Neel Shivane (7)	8
Ethan Westwood (6)	9
Bethany Liddicoat (7)	10
Owen Hill (6)	11
John Mercer (7)	12
Taylor Waterfield (6)	13
Tommy Mellor (6)	14
George William Robert Sutton (6)	15
Blake McGarry (6)	16
Jack Evans (6)	17
Ewan Paice (6)	18
Daniel Gurney (7)	19
Sarah Osborne (6)	20
Lacie Isla Tucker (6)	21
Ethan Cragg (7)	22
Zac Hitchcock (6)	23
Riley Temlett (6)	24
Isla Fisher (7)	25
Clayton Ruiz (6)	26
William Tasker (6)	27

Blackhorse Primary School, Bristol

George Adams (7)	28
Isabelle Margaret Rothwell (7)	29
Oscar Mustoe (6)	30
Sophia Jones (6)	31
Adelyn Calvert (6)	32
Erin Daniel (6)	33
Grace Taylor (6)	34
Amelia Unthank (7)	35
Bethany Winter (6)	36
Lorena Maggie Stock (7)	37
Evelyn Blackburn (6)	38
Louis Clarke (7)	39
Jack Williamson (6)	40
Sarah Allan (6)	41
Kai Hurley (6)	42
Lucy Jane Dempster (7)	43
Josiah Latham (6)	44
Jack Oliver Leather (6)	45
Patrick Harris (6)	46
Lucy Wright (6)	47
Kyran Blackmore-Mead (6)	48
Shayaan Amin (7)	49
Millie May Pope (6)	50
Matthew Thomas Friend (7)	51
Jack Stuart Clancy (7)	52
Ayaan Rafiq (7)	53
Mitchell David Daniel Evans-Rice (6)	54
Adam Reed (6)	55
Jack Luxton (6)	56
Amelie Russ (6)	57
Liam McDonagh-Langley (7)	58
Luke John Clancy (7)	59

Chagford CE Primary School, Newton Abbot

Maisie-Jayne Summer Simons (7)	60
Isla Barrau (6)	61
Charlotte Garratt (6)	62
Olivia Waterfall (6)	63
Kitty McDiarmid (6)	64
Ember Hine (6)	65
Charlotte Rose H (6)	66
Poppy Lola Dooley-Cloke (6)	67
Gryffin Gordon Clark (6)	68
Anastasia Elizabeth Leaman (6)	69
Lily Grace Sargent (6)	70
Charlie Mathewson-Coombe (6)	71
Noah Tarbet (7)	72
Lewis Edward Henry Litwinski (6)	73
Matthew Cooper (8)	74
Junior Andrew Mackenzie (6)	75
Harry Thynne (6)	76

Cheddar Grove Primary School, Bristol

Karson Jay Densley (5)	77
Lucie Phillips (6)	78
Lillie-May Allen (5)	80
Emily Rose Newman (6)	81
Samuel Medway (6)	82
Mason Chick (6)	83
Ella Grace Baxter (6)	84
Autumn Clothier (7)	85
Demi Selway (6)	86
Jessica Louise Simmons (7)	87
Molly Rogers (6)	88
Charlie Brice (6)	89
Brendon Kelly (6)	90
Alfie Barber (6)	91
Isabella Muscat (6)	92
Alice Gommo (6)	93
Oliver West (5)	94
Lottie Cartwright (6)	95
Gracie-Lou Cornish (5)	96
Sonny Alfie Kibby (6)	97

Lacey Gillett (5)	98
Leon Green (6)	99
Alexa Lowe Wilson-Rawlings (6)	100
Charlotte Hill (5)	101
Mariah Curtis (6)	102
Holly Martin (5)	103
Harmony McGauley (5)	104
Millie Brookman (5)	105
Harry Scott Gribble (6)	106
Miley Rose Gazzard (6)	107
Davi Egho (6)	108
Finley Forristal (6)	109
Alfie Hazell (6)	110
Archie Isom (5)	111
Harrison Edward Govier (6)	112
Frankie Baker (5)	113
Ruby Jones (5)	114
Lucy-Lei Katrina Campho (6)	115
Ellis Pitman (7)	116
Justin Cove (6)	117
Dylan Noel (6)	118
Zackary Daniel Brice (5)	119
Naomi Allen (5)	120
Lennon Ross Govier (6)	121
Freya Jones (5)	122
Jessica Evans (6)	123
Caroline Mark Hazell (5)	124
Beau Hickery (5)	125
Brooke Turner (5)	126
Lily Avril Callen (6)	127
Liam Dunn (5)	128
Jude Clark (5)	129
Shay Goff (7)	130
Ria Ashley Williamson (5)	131
Willow Young (5)	132
Lily May (5)	133
Tahlia Zylinska (5)	134
Albert Delahunty (6)	135
Dylan Colgan (6)	136
Megan Allen (5)	137
Ava Carnevale (5)	138
Callum Colgan (6)	139
Woody Milkins (6)	140
Harley Court (5)	141

King's Park Academy, Bournemouth

Tayah Lawrence-Decker (5)	142
Alicja Damasiewicz (5)	143
Marcie Goodchild (6)	144
Sebastian Andrei Bran (5)	145
Ethan Frampton (5)	146
João Serrao (5)	147
Daisy Smee (5)	148
Kelly De Sousa (5)	149
Patryk Mitera (5)	150
Oliver Fay (5)	151
Zuzanna Jakubowska (6)	152
Samuel Lee Edensor (5)	153
Nicole Lipka (5)	154
Alexander Wilson (5)	155

Trinity CE (VA) First School, Verwood

Grace Poole (7)	156

The Stories

Olivier's Pirate Story

One sunny day, Emma and Ben were walking the dog. Suddenly, the dog started barking at a magic door hidden in a tree.

The dog found treasure in a big pile and a big coconut tree.

The a big, scary and creepy pirate said, 'That is my treasure.'

Ben said, 'We found this treasure first.'

'Ha, ha, it is mine now!'

'Hey, that's not fair, I found it first.'

Ben slipped off the plank.

Ben landed on a kind dolphin with the dog and Emma landed on a dolphin.

The dolphins got them back home to the tree house and Emma and Ben said, 'High five!'

Olivier Kalinowski (6)

Blackhorse Primary School, Bristol

Rihanna's Superhero Story

... Superhero Land!

Emma and Ben were superheroes!

They were amazed and they tried to fly. They did!

It was amazing but it wasn't long until something black caught their eye.

They looked down and saw a robber.

So Emma, Ben and their dog flew down and said, 'Stop, or we will drag you along to prison!'

So they did and the robber said, 'You will pay for this!'

But Emma and Ben just said, 'We will never pay, robber.'

When they got back to where they started, they suddenly found some medals on their chests.

Soon, it was getting late and it was nearly teatime, so they went to the door and walked through.

They ran back home.

Rihanna Andrews (7)

Bickleigh Down CE Primary School, Plymouth

Isabel's Magical Story

... a beautiful castle.

'Look,' said Emma, 'a castle.'

Ben asked, 'Should we go inside?'

Emma was very scared. 'Are you sure?'

'Yes,' said Ben.

Ben and Emma saw a fairy. She said, 'Where are you going?' Ben said that they were just having a look. The fairy cried and said, 'But this is my castle.'

'Oh,' said Emma.

Then behind Ben there was a troll. 'Hello everyone,' said the troll.

Ben said, 'You look ugly.'

'No, I am not.'

'Let's celebrate,' said the troll. 'I wanted to show you my house today because it's nearly Christmas.' In the house, the troll said, 'Let's have a party.'

Emma and Ben were very tired.

But Ben and Emma were very pleased.

Isabel Joshy (6)
Bickleigh Down CE Primary School, Plymouth

3

Sienna's Magical Story

... a magical fairy castle. Ben and Emma were so surprised. Just then, they heard a quiet sound.
It was a fairy from the magical castle. Emma said to the fairy, 'What's wrong?'
The fairy said, 'A troll is having a party, but I can't get there because I lost my powers.'
So Emma and Ben helped the fairy get to the troll's party in time. When they got there, the troll was waiting. Emma and Ben were scared when they saw the troll.
The troll let them in. Emma and Ben weren't scared of the troll anymore and the troll had a candy house.
The party was fun. Emma and Ben didn't want to go. At the party they had a cake, party hats and presents.
Then it was time to go. Emma and Ben said goodbye and went back home. They had a piece of cake.

Sienna Martin (6)
Bickleigh Down CE Primary School, Plymouth

Lilia's Magical Story

... a magical land.

Emma gasped. 'I love it!' she said.

They saw a huge, leafy castle.

They opened the door and saw a fairy. Then she disappeared. She appeared on a mushroom. The fairy said, 'Hi, I'm Tinkerbell.'

'Hi,' said Emma.

'Hi,' said Ben.

The fairy said, 'Follow me.' So they did. She led them to a troll.

'My name is Jack Frost,' said the troll. 'Come to my yummy house.'

Jack Frost led them to his house.

'It's a gingerbread house!' shouted Ben and Emma.

'Come in,' said Jack Frost.

Inside the house there was a fairy. They set up a party and had a party. It was getting late so they said goodbye to Tinkerbell and Jack Frost and they went home laughing.

Lilia Kilpatrick (7)
Bickleigh Down CE Primary School, Plymouth

Isla's Magical Story

... a magical place!
Emma and Ben said, 'Wow, it's amazing.'
Soon, they saw a castle. 'It's nice,' Emma said to Ben.
'Ooh ahh,' he said.
Then Emma and Ben saw a fairy. 'Hello, I'm Emma.'
'And I'm Ben.'
'Oh,' said the fairy.
'Oh,' said Ben and Emma.
With the fairy, Emma and Ben soon met a stinky troll and he was disgusting and stupid. 'Hello,' said all three.
'Hello,' said the troll deeply to Emma, Ben and the fairy. 'Come and have candy from my house.'
'Oh!' shouted Emma and Ben.
'OK,' said the fairy in a small voice on a mushroom.
Emma and Ben had a great time.
So they said goodbye and left. They went home.

Isla Stringer (6)
Bickleigh Down CE Primary School, Plymouth

Troy's Superhero Story

... Superhero World! Emma and Ben turned into superheroes. They loved it. They flew to the sky. In the sky, they saw a villain so they flew down to the ground and Emma and Ben ran to catch the burglar.

They took the villain to their station and said, 'What have you stolen?'

He said, 'I haven't stolen anything.'

But Emma and Ben and the dog saw the villain's sack.

Emma and Ben chucked the villain into jail and super Emma and super Ben and super dog smiled. Super Emma and super Ben and super dog got a big medal and everybody cheered.

Super Emma and super Ben and super dog flew back to the magical door underneath the tree.

Troy Johnson (7)
Bickleigh Down CE Primary School, Plymouth

Neel's Space Story

... space! Emma and Ben were floating with stars. Soon, they landed on the planet Venus.

Emma and Ben jumped around on Venus. It was fun. But they did not notice the alien.

Then they felt something flying above them and they looked up. They saw the alien and he pulled them in.

Emma and Ben made good friends with the alien and the dog loved the ship. They were all really happy and smiling.

Then, *whoosh!* A monster tongue tipped the ship, but they fought back. They kept getting tipped back and forth.

Soon, the battle finished and they had won. So they were saved and went back home.

Neel Shivane (7)

Bickleigh Down CE Primary School, Plymouth

Ethan's Pirate Story

... Pirate Land!

'Pirate land!' said Emma and Ben, surprised.

Suddenly, Emma and Ben went to Drake's Island and there was a box with lots of treasure in it and on it

Suddenly, a naughty pirate called Captain Hook laughed and said, 'I want my treasure.'

They got to the Jolly Roger. They said, 'Walk the plank at once!'

'Dolphins will save us,' said the two children with a smile.

Then they said, 'Run, run as fast as you can because you can't catch us!'

Ethan Westwood (6)
Bickleigh Down CE Primary School, Plymouth

Bethany's Superhero Story

... Superhero Land! Emma and Ben turned into superheroes! They were amazed this happened. Emma and Ben flew into the air.
They stopped for a moment and underneath their feet there was a robber.
Emma and Ben flew down to the ground and caught the robber. 'Stop right there!' they both said. 'Otherwise, you're going to prison.'
They threw him into prison and he was locked up.
'Another day saved,' they both said together.
After that, they flew back to the magic door.

Bethany Liddicoat (7)
Bickleigh Down CE Primary School, Plymouth

Owen's Superhero Story

... Superhero Land! One day, Emma and Ben were flying in the sky. They were having so much fun. But there was a robber that Emma and Ben couldn't see. The robber had a sack full of money from the bank.

Then Emma and Ben saw the robber and phoned the cops. The cops were on their way. Then he got arrested.

The cops put the big, bad robber in prison.

Then they saved the bank once again. I bet they are the best superheroes ever!

So the best heroes, Emma and Ben, flew back home to have a rest.

Owen Hill (6)

Bickleigh Down CE Primary School, Plymouth

John's Jungle Story

... a jungle! In the jungle there were slippery ropes and that's what they landed on.

The ropes led them to a hard branch with a scary snake on it.

They noticed that it was a scary snake so they ran away.

Next, they came to a lion after the snake lost them.

They noticed that it was a friendly lion, so they rode on him.

It was so fast that they fell off and got picked up by the slippery ropes.

They saw the magic door again and it led them back home.

John Mercer (7)

Bickleigh Down CE Primary School, Plymouth

Taylor's Magical Story

... a magical land! In the magical land there was a castle. The castle was huge. Ben and Emma were surprised.

Ben and Emma saw a fairy sitting on a mushroom. The fairy told them to see a smelly troll.

They saw a smelly troll. The smelly troll told them to go to a gingerbread house.

The troll took them to a scrumptious gingerbread house.

Ben and Emma had a party to celebrate the wonderful magic.

Then they went home with lots of lovely presents.

Taylor Waterfield (6)

Bickleigh Down CE Primary School, Plymouth

Tommy's Superhero Story

... a planet and they looked down. Then they stopped for a minute.

Soon, Ben saw a robber. Ben said, 'Emma, a robber!'

Ben and Emma floated down, then they went on the ground. They ran as fast as they could.

Ben and Emma went to a dead-end to catch the robber. They walked to the robber.

That was the end of the robber.

Ben and Emma and the dog got an award.

Then Ben and Emma and the dog went in the magic door.

Tommy Mellor (6)
Bickleigh Down CE Primary School, Plymouth

George's Jungle Story

... The jungle!

'What on Earth are we doing here?' said Ben.

Soon they met a snake. Emma and Ben were terrified of the snake and the snake said, 'I'm a good snake.'

He was lying. Emma and Ben were running as fast as they could.

They met a lion. The lion said, 'I can help you?'

'Hop on and I'll take you home,' said the lion.

At last they were home like nothing had happened.

George William Robert Sutton (6)

Bickleigh Down CE Primary School, Plymouth

Blake's Magical Story

... a magical world. They saw a castle. The castle was giant and big. The castle had a gate. They wanted to go inside with their dog.
They saw a fairy with big, brown wings.
Then they saw an ugly troll. He was ugly but nice.
He took them to a gingerbread house and the troll let them eat the house. The dog had a candy cane. Then they had a party to celebrate.
They came out of the door hidden in the tree and went home.

Blake McGarry (6)
Bickleigh Down CE Primary School, Plymouth

Jack's Superhero Story

... Superhero Land!

A robber ran out of the bank with lots of money and he smiled.

'After him!' said Ben.

'Stop right there. What have you done?'

'I robbed a bank.'

'You're going to prison.'

'Thanks for catching him,' said the police.

'You're welcome.'

'Now we party. Protect the pride land,' said Ben.

'Let's go back.'

Jack Evans (6)

Bickleigh Down CE Primary School, Plymouth

Ewan's Jungle Story

... a jungle! They swung and swung until they flew off. They landed on a tree branch.

Ben and Emma met a snake and were scared. They ran fast.

They ran and ran and ran quite fast until the snake almost caught them.

They saw a lion and made friends. The lion helped them out.

They got on the lion and the lion ran quicker than the snake.

Emma and Ben swung until they got through the magic door.

Ewan Paice (6)
Bickleigh Down CE Primary School, Plymouth

Daniel's Magical Story

... a magical island! Then, they ran to the castle. After that, they opened the door and saw a fairy! Then she disappeared and had a ride on the dog! Then the dog tipped her off.

Then all of them saw a monster who said, 'You can come to my house.' Then they followed him.

When they went inside, they had a party. They had balloons and party hats. They went home and told their mum.

Daniel Gurney (7)
Bickleigh Down CE Primary School, Plymouth

Sarah's Superhero Story

... Superhero Land! They flew through the air in double quick time.

Just then, Emma spotted a robber. 'Stop!' she shouted.

'Never!' was the reply.

They flew down. Ben shouted, 'Stop and give that bag to me!'

They flung the robber in jail with a crash.

'We've done it again,' they said.

Then they flew back home for a rest.

Sarah Osborne (6)
Bickleigh Down CE Primary School, Plymouth

Lacie's Superhero Story

... Superhero Land!

One day, Emma and Ben were superheroes. They loved flying with their pet.

The next day, they saw that their magic was gone because they saw a robber.

Emma and Ben jumped out of the window to catch him quickly.

Then they took him to the dungeons. Then they flew out.

They saved the day and everyone cheered.

Then they flew home.

Lacie Isla Tucker (6)
Bickleigh Down CE Primary School, Plymouth

Ethan's Space Story

... space. Emma and Ben were running.
Emma and Ben were pointing at the stars. The alien saw them.
He flew a rocket on top of Ben and Emma's heads.
They zoomed up in a light and they made friends with the alien.
There was a monster blowing them underneath the space rocket. They were all worried.
They got out of the space rocket and said goodbye.

Ethan Cragg (7)
Bickleigh Down CE Primary School, Plymouth

Zac's Superhero Story

... Superland. Emma and Ben were superheroes with a super dog.

Ben and Emma were superheroes and they were catching a bad guy.

Emma and Ben were cross with the baddie because he hurt people and stole money from them.

Ben put the baddie in prison.

Ben and Emma were superheroes.

They went back to the secret door in the tree.

Zac Hitchcock (6)
Bickleigh Down CE Primary School, Plymouth

Riley's Superhero Story

... Super World.

They saw a robber stealing money. They followed him. He ran and ran to his lair.

Super Emma and Super Ben and Super Dog caught him.

They put the robber in jail. That was the end of him.

Super Emma and Super Ben and Super Dog saved the world again.

They went home.

Riley Temlett (6)
Bickleigh Down CE Primary School, Plymouth

Isla's Magical Story

... a magical world. Soon, they saw a wonderland.
The dog barked and they saw a fairy.
The fairy said, 'Two of us go to the troll.'
They were terrified and they said no.
Then the troll led them to his house.
They had a party and home time came.
And so they left.

Isla Fisher (7)
Bickleigh Down CE Primary School, Plymouth

Clayton's Superhero Story

... Superhero Land. They caught a robber.
The robber ran away. He was carrying a huge bag.
Finally, they caught him.
Then he was in jail. He was sad and he felt bad.
Then Ben and Emma did an outstanding superhero pose.
Ben and Emma strike again!

Clayton Ruiz (6)
Bickleigh Down CE Primary School, Plymouth

William's Space Story

... space! When they were in space they saw aliens.
They were on their own planet.
Then they got abducted!
It was fine because the aliens were saving them from a monster!
They just got in!
Then they went to find the door home.

William Tasker (6)
Bickleigh Down CE Primary School, Plymouth

George's Superhero Story

Ben and Emma opened the door and it took them to a beautiful, magical land. They were so surprised. Ben became Hulk and Emma was Supergirl. Ben could throw rocks 20 whole miles and Emma could do tricks in the air.

One day, a robber came. He tried to steal the king's precious crown but then Hulk had a battle with the sneaky robber. He was really fast and Hulk couldn't catch him. He ran to his car and drove away.

Then Supergirl flew so fast. Supergirl caught him and they had a little talk about stealing. The king got his crown back. Hulk and Supergirl called 999. The robber went to jail for two years. All he could do was read a book. He hated books, except books that said how he should steal stuff without getting caught.

After they saved the day, they were awarded by the police and they felt really happy that they saved the day like real superheroes.

Then they went back home to their superhero tree and they couldn't wait for their next adventure.

George Adams (7)
Blackhorse Primary School, Bristol

Isabelle's Superhero Story

Ben and Emma opened the door and it took them to a beautiful fun land and they looked down. They were so surprised that they started to fly. Then they flew down.

Suddenly, they saw a robber. Ben and Emma saw a sack on his back. They wondered what was in it. Maybe it was gold treasure.

Suddenly, Ben and Emma shouted, 'Stop!' but he tricked them so they used their superpowers to get him.

'You can't catch me!'

'Yes, we can.'

'Yes, we caught him, I knew we would.'

'Nooo! I don't want to be in jail.' The robber didn't want to be in jail but he had to stay there forever.

'We saved the day.' The dog, Ben and Emma were so happy that they saved the day. They are a team of superheroes, including the dog.

So they used their superpowers to fly home to their super home with their dog, Burtie, and there was no more stealing.

Isabelle Margaret Rothwell (7)

Blackhorse Primary School, Bristol

Oscar's Pirate Story

... a boat on the sea. They were worried for a minute, then they noticed an island and rowed towards it. They got there and got off the boat. They found a treasure chest on the island and opened it. They saw gold, thousands of gold coins, and started to help themselves.

Then a pirate got off his ship and captured them.

'Argh!' screamed Ben.

'Let me go!' shouted Emma.

'No,' said the pirate.

The pirate made them work for him for a bit and made them work hard. Then he made them walk the plank. But then they saw something. What do you think they saw?

Two friendly dolphins came along and they sailed away on the dolphins. But the pirate was chasing them, so they made a hole in the ship and it sank. Ben and Emma went back through the tree. They pretended they were pirates and played together. They had fun.

Oscar Mustoe (6)

Blackhorse Primary School, Bristol

Sophia's Superhero Story

Ben and Emma opened the door and it took them to a robber. They turned into superheroes. One of them was Spidergirl and one was Batman. They found a dog and he turned into a superhero.

They found the robber again, so they jumped into the air and started to fly. They caught the sneaky robber, so they went somewhere else.

They said, 'What were you doing?' They took him to a police station and they put him behind some bars.

'We have had a big day, so let's go to bed early,' said Spidergirl.

'Let's go to our home,' said Batman. 'C'mon, Superdog.'

'Come on,' said Spidergirl, 'we are almost there now.'

'Here we are, Superdog, here's your new home,' said Spidergirl.

'Come on,' said Batman.

'Superdog, get inside,' said Spidergirl.

Sophia Jones (6)

Blackhorse Primary School, Bristol

Adelyn's Superhero Story

Ben and Emma opened the door and it took them to a beautiful land. When they looked down, they were shocked as they had become superheroes! Suddenly, they saw a robber. He was running away. He had the Queen's jewels so they chased him but he ran up a hill and it was too slidey to catch him.

Luckily, they caught him and stopped him from getting away. The little dog grabbed the robber's leg.

They put him in jail and everyone cheered. They gave the superheroes medals. They made them their superheroes.

The superheroes let them have an autograph and they were the world's best heroes. They were in every newspaper.

After lunch, they flew back to the tree and headed home.

'Well, that was an adventure,' said Emma.

'Yes it was, now let's go home,' said Ben.

Adelyn Calvert (6)

Blackhorse Primary School, Bristol

Erin's Superhero Story

Ben and Emma opened the door and it took them to the open air. Emma and Ben didn't know that they were superheroes, but then they did because they were flying.

Then they met a robber. He was a nasty robber, he stole everything. He ran to Emma and Ben and talked and talked.

Suddenly, he started to shout, 'You get away, you nasty people.' He had a ring in his hand.

They said, 'Where did you steal that ring from?'

'A wedding,' he said.

The robber was fed up with going to jail. He shouted to try to get out.

Eventually, they got the robber in jail after all. They got a reward from the police.

They loved being superheroes. The dog was surprised that he was a superhero dog.

Erin Daniel (6)

Blackhorse Primary School, Bristol

Grace's Superhero Story

Ben and Emma opened the door and it took them to a beautiful funland. They looked down and they were so surprised because they had superhero suits on and they were flying.

Suddenly, they saw a robber with a sack with golden rings and crowns in it. Then he tripped over. Suddenly, they picked him up and said, 'Stop! or we will put you in jail.'

'But you can't catch me!'

'Yes, we can.'

'Yes, we caught him. I knew we would catch him.'

'I don't want to be in jail.'

'Yes, we saved the day. We're superheroes and so is the dog.'

They went in the magic door. They went home and lived happily ever after.

Grace Taylor (6)
Blackhorse Primary School, Bristol

Amelia's Superhero Story

Ben and Emma opened the door and it took them to a fabulous world. They didn't know what they were wearing, but then Emma realised what she was wearing. 'It's superhero clothes,' she said.

A robber came along and stole the Queen's jewels. Then Ben saw the robber.

They caught him with a net and had a talk to him, but he didn't say anything back. Eventually, they made him talk.

He got put in prison. He tried to break out but he couldn't, so he left it.

All three of them got a rosette and a trophy. They went looking for more annoyances.

They came out of the door and their family ran up to them and gave them a hug.

Amelia Unthank (7)
Blackhorse Primary School, Bristol

Bethany's Pirate Story

When Emma and Ben opened the door, they found a brown boat. The dog started barking again. Ben said, 'I think he wants us to go in the boat.'
In the distance, Emma and Ben saw an island and on that island was a treasure chest.
But when Emma and Ben were looking at all the shiny, glittery and sparkly treasure, a pirate saw them.
Then the pirate grabbed them and took them to his ship. Ben said, 'Let us go!'
But the pirate said, 'No, go and walk the plank!'
Then a dolphin came and Emma and Ben jumped on and went 'Wheeee!'
When Ben and Emma went home, they said, 'I'm glad we're home.'

Bethany Winter (6)

Blackhorse Primary School, Bristol

Lorena's Pirate Story

One day there lived a girl called Emma and a boy called Ben. They took their dog for a walk and found a boat. They were very happy and the dog was happy too.

When they all got off the boat, the dog saw a treasure chest, so Emma jumped up and down on the treasure chest, but it would not open.

Then suddenly, a big, bad pirate came and opened the treasure chest with his sword. He took Emma, Ben and the dog to his boat.

Captain Hook said, 'Go and walk the plank or you will be sorry!'

But when the dolphins saw the boy walking the plank, they saved them.

When they got home, they ran in and sat down.

Lorena Maggie Stock (7)
Blackhorse Primary School, Bristol

Evelyn's Superhero Story

Emma and Ben opened the door and it took them to Superhero Land. Then they looked down and saw that they were flying.

Then they saw a robber, so they swooped down and caught him. The dog bit him so they caught the sack.

Then they started to tell him off. He was sneaking off and they caught him so they used some superpowers.

They took him to jail. He felt bad for himself, then he started to cry.

Emma and Ben felt like real superheroes and they got some medals from the king and queen.

Then they went back to the secret door. They went back through the tree and back to their real home.

Evelyn Blackburn (6)
Blackhorse Primary School, Bristol

Louis' Superhero Story

Ben and Emma opened the door and it took them to Brean Leisure Park. They were jumping up and down so much that it made them into superheroes! Then they saw a robber who had stolen somebody's handbag and purse.

They caught the robber. He shouldn't have stolen the handbag and purse,
so they put him in jail.

They told the robber that he had to stay in jail for as many days as the police said.

Then they got their medals. That's how they became superheroes.

Then they went home for tea and they were superheroes forever.

Louis Clarke (7)

Blackhorse Primary School, Bristol

Jack's Pirate Story

Have you ever been on a boat? Do you want to?
Well, read on to find out more about pirates.
Emma was standing on a chest of jewels and coins
and smiling because she found treasure.
They found Jack Sparrow and thought he could
help them get away. He did and they got away.
Jack Sparrow made them walk the plank and they
did walk the plank. There were two dolphins who
came to help.
The dolphins came and they got on them. In a
flash, they got home and had tea.
They got home and went to sleep. They got up and
had another adventure.

Jack Williamson (6)
Blackhorse Primary School, Bristol

Sarah's Superhero Story

They opened the door and Emma and Ben were superheroes. They saw their wonderful capes and bright costumes.

A robber came and was stealing people's money, so the heroes were in action.

They shot down and caught him, but he threw the money. The heroes caught the money and gave it back to the people.

They said that he should go in jail, so he had a year to think about his behaviour.

All of the country was so proud of Emma and Ben, so they got a rosette.

They flew into the magic door and they were safe in their cosy beds.

Sarah Allan (6)
Blackhorse Primary School, Bristol

Kai's Pirate Story

... a pirate world. There was a mean pirate. He was the captain and he was called Big Bad Pirate. He was the meanest pirate in the world!
On Pirate World there was a map. They found the big map then, Big Bad Pirate gave them a treasure chest but it had a boxing glove.
Then Emma and Ben found another treasure chest. Then the pirate got his sword out and he chopped his head off. Oops!
Then they walked the plank. Luckily, dolphins caught them.
Then they had a ride home.
When they went home, they lived happily ever after.

Kai Hurley (6)
Blackhorse Primary School, Bristol

Lucy's Pirate Story

... a pirate island. They saw an island and sailed to it. They saw something and went towards it.

They saw some treasure and Emma played with it, but then she saw a pirate ship.

A pirate came towards them and he took them to his ship. He made Ben walk the plank.

Ben walked the plank, but something appeared in Ben's eye. It was a dolphin.

The dolphins gave them a ride across the seven seas and back to the magic door.

They went through the magic door and never told their mum about it. They lived happily ever after.

Lucy Jane Dempster (7)
Blackhorse Primary School, Bristol

Josiah's Pirate Story

Ben, Emma and their dog found themselves on a ship. They saw an island and they sailed towards it. Ben, Emma and the dog found treasure and they played with it. Then they saw a pirate ship.
The pirate swashbuckled them back to the ship. The ship was old, wooden and rusty.
Then he made them walk the plank. Two dolphins came and rescued them.
They rode back playfully on the dolphins. The dolphins laughed and they laughed.
They ran home and Emma, Ben and the dog laughed. They played in the park before they went home.

Josiah Latham (6)
Blackhorse Primary School, Bristol

Jack's Superhero Story

Ben and Emma found a secret door and they went in it. They realised that they were now superheroes.

The robber was escaping the prison. Hulk was so mad, he jumped really high.

The robber found the two superheroes and Hulk was raging mad. He used his superpowers.

They took the robber to jail and they called the police. They were especially happy about that.

They were so happy, even Bertie was happy because of Emma and Ben.

They went off and they were so proud of themselves. Bertie was panting because it was so hot.

Jack Oliver Leather (6)

Blackhorse Primary School, Bristol

Patrick's Pirate Story

Ben rowed the boat. The dog barked. The dog saw an island.

Ben saw the island and he steered the boat to the island. When they got to the island, they saw treasure.

Emma, Ben and their dog met a nice, lovely and generous pirate. The pirate wanted to help them. The pirate told them his name. He was called Jack Sparrow. He told them to jump on the dolphins' backs.

When the children got on the dolphins' backs, the dolphins took them back to shore.

'Bye-bye,' said Ben. Away they went to the door.

Patrick Harris (6)
Blackhorse Primary School, Bristol

Lucy's Superhero Story

Emma and Ben opened the door and it took them to a power land. The next time they looked down, they realised they were wearing superhero outfits. They were having fun, then they saw a robber.
They flew down and caught the robber. They said, 'Oi, you can't rule the world!'
So they called the police and they put him in jail, never to be seen again.
The police gave them all medals. They stood on the crest of the highest mountain they could find.
They flew right down and went back through the door.

Lucy Wright (6)
Blackhorse Primary School, Bristol

Kyran's Superhero Story

Ben and Emma pushed the door and it took them to Superhero Land. They were Superman and Supergirl and Superdog.
The Joker was robbing the bank. The superheroes surrounded him and the dog was growling at him.
'Why are you robbing the bank? That is wrong,' said Superman.
'Help, I'm sorry.'
'But like I said, that is wrong, that's why you're going in jail.'
The superheroes got badges from the police.
'Let's go,' said Superman.
Off they flew back home.

Kyran Blackmore-Mead (6)
Blackhorse Primary School, Bristol

Shayaan's Superhero Story

Ben and Emma opened the door and it took them to a magic land. It turned them into The Flash and Superwoman and Flash Dog.

They saw a robber so they chased after him. Flash and Flash Dog were too fast so they caught him.

They said to the robber, 'Give me the bag.'

'No.'

'I am going to take your mask off if you don't give it to us.'

'No,' said the robber.

But then the police came and put him in jail.

Ben and Emma went back.

They went home.

Shayaan Amin (7)

Blackhorse Primary School, Bristol

Millie's Pirate Story

... an island. It was a beautiful island full of coconut trees. Ben shouted, 'A boat!' so they rowed to an island.

On the island there was a treasure chest. Emma saw a crown and put it on.

In the distance, Ben could see a pirate ship.

The pirate made them walk the plank.

Some friendly dolphins came and gave Ben and Emma a ride on their backs.

'That was great!' said Ben.

'You're right,' said Emma.

Then they went back through the magic door.

Millie May Pope (6)
Blackhorse Primary School, Bristol

Matthew's Superhero Story

Emma and Ben went through a door and it took them to a school. Ben looked down and he saw they had new clothes.

Emma told Ben she could see a robber. They saw the robber steal 100 books, 20 children and money and 225 pencils.

Ben told the robber, 'Why do I think you stole 100 books, 20 children and money and 225 pencils?'

Ben told the robber to stay in jail for 100 years.

Team Ben saved Wales and France and the whole wide world.

They flew through the magic door.

Matthew Thomas Friend (7)

Blackhorse Primary School, Bristol

Jack's Superhero Story

Ben and Emma opened the door and it took them to Crazy Land. They jumped and they found out that they had super powers. They could throw massive rocks really far.

They saw a thief robbing a bank. He got away so they looked and looked, but they couldn't find him. They found the criminal who robbed the bank and they caught him.

He went to jail and he was in jail for the rest of his life.

They were really happy that they saved the world.

Jack Stuart Clancy (7)
Blackhorse Primary School, Bristol

Ayaan's Pirate Story

Emma and Ben were falling down the sky. Ben held tightly onto the dog. They landed on a boat. Meanwhile, they saw an island and it had trees on it. They even found treasure. Ben saw a pirate ship. The pirates got off the ship. A mean pirate called Captain Flubber took them on the ship.

Captain Flubber threw them in the sea. 'Oh no!' said Emma.

Then they had a dolphin ride.

Soon, they went home and lived happily ever after.

Ayaan Rafiq (7)
Blackhorse Primary School, Bristol

Mitchell's Pirate Story

Ben and Emma fell in a boat in the middle of the sea. There was a pirate so far away.
Next, they found gold, so then the pirates came and they got taken away.
They hid but the pirates found them. They took them to the boat.
The pirate said, 'Get off and walk the plank.'
Two dolphins came to save them, so they swam away.
They got back home to the real world with their pet.

Mitchell David Daniel Evans-Rice (6)
Blackhorse Primary School, Bristol

Adam's Superhero Story

Emma and Ben opened the door and became superheroes. Ben was Hulk and Emma was Hulk Woman.

There was a robber. Hulk Ben made a diamond with a bomb and *bang!*

The bomb didn't work so they both smashed him.

The robber went in jail for 20 weeks. He was so sad.

Emma and Ben were so happy that they defeated the robber.

Emma and Ben went home to a super house.

Adam Reed (6)

Blackhorse Primary School, Bristol

Jack's Pirate Story

The door took Ben and Emma to an adventure.
They landed on a boat, then they found treasure.
Emma dressed up like a queen.
Then pirates found them and took them. 'Arr, me
hearties,' said a pirate.
The pirates told them to walk the plank.
Then dolphins came so they had a ride.
Then they went back to California.

Jack Luxton (6)
Blackhorse Primary School, Bristol

Amelie's Pirate Story

Have you ever been on a boat? Do you get seasick? The boat is really nice and it floats.
Emma and Ben found some coins and a nice, beautiful chest.
A man came to get the treasure, but he was a pirate.
The pirate made them walk the plank.
Then they had a ride on dolphins. They didn't get wet.
They got home safely.

Amelie Russ (6)
Blackhorse Primary School, Bristol

Liam's Pirate Story

One sunny day, they found a door hidden in a tree, so they went to see it.
Then they found a chest.
They found a boat and a pirate on the boat.
The pirate made the children walk the plank.
Some dolphins came to rescue the children.
The children escaped on the dolphins with the dog.

Liam McDonagh-Langley (7)

Blackhorse Primary School, Bristol

Luke's Pirate Story

They were sailing in the sea. They spotted an island.

They saw a treasure chest full of gold but then they saw a pirate ship.

Suddenly, a pirate spotted them.

The pirate made them walk the plank.

Two kind dolphins gave them a ride.

They rushed home through a magic door.

Luke John Clancy (7)

Blackhorse Primary School, Bristol

Maisie's Magical Story

Once upon a time in a magical land, Ben and Emma were walking their cute bulldog on a sunny day by a tree. There was a door in the tree.

Next, they saw a magical, sparkly, shiny fairy sitting on the step. 'Hello,' said Tinkerbell. 'What do you want?'

Next, Ben, Emma and the dog said, 'We just wondered what was behind the door.'

Then a goblin came out. 'Hello,' he said. 'Would you like to visit my ginger house?'

'Yes please,' said Ben, Emma and the dog.

'Let's have a great, massive party.'

'Okay then. I will get the party hats,' Ben said.

'I will get the balloons,' said Emma, 'and we can start the party.'

At the end, Ben, Emma and the dog said thank you and they went home.

Maisie-Jayne Summer Simons (7)
Chagford CE Primary School, Newton Abbot

Isla's Jungle Story

... a jungle. At first, they didn't know what to do. They saw some vines so they started swinging. When they stopped swinging, they jumped off. When they jumped off, the dog started to bark at a snake. The children looked terrified because they were scared.

The snake began to chase the children, so the children started to run away.

The children stopped running because they ran out of breath. When they stopped, they saw a lion. They looked frightened but the lion said nice things.

The children asked the lion, 'Can you get us home?' The lion said, 'Yes.'

They saw the vines so they started to swing. When they stopped, they saw the door. When Emma and Ben opened the door, it took them home.

Isla Barrau (6)

Chagford CE Primary School, Newton Abbot

Charlotte's Pirate Story

One sunny day, Emma and Ben were running towards a boat to look for treasure because their mum would like jewellery.

Emma and Ben jumped in the boat and got to the treasure. But Emma and Ben didn't see the pirates coming.

The pirates jumped and Emma and Ben got scared. So they stood back but when they stood back, they fell in the boat.

When they got on the boat, Ben ran on the diving board. Then Emma ran and they jumped onto the dolphins.

They had a race and they saw a very nice view. They went past the boat.

When they went past the boat, they took off the hats and ran past a tree. They didn't see a door in the tree.

Charlotte Garratt (6)

Chagford CE Primary School, Newton Abbot

Olivia's Jungle Story

... a jungle. The jungle was big and angry because it had been woken up. Soon it was full of noises. The first animal they saw was a snake. It had big, beady eyes and had a tangled tail. Emma and Ben looked worried and that helped the snake. It chased them but soon it was out of sight. Soon they were in lots of bushes.

It was while they were there that they met a lion. It was a nice lion.

It gave them a ride. When they got off, they jumped onto a vine.

When they got off, they saw the door. Emma said, 'We must get back.'

But Ben said, 'Can't we go on a quick walk?'

'Yes,' said Emma.

Olivia Waterfall (6)

Chagford CE Primary School, Newton Abbot

Kitty's Jungle Story

Emma and Ben found themselves in a jungle! They said, 'Cool, I've always wanted to live in a jungle.'
'*Woof*', said the dog.

But then they came to a massive, scaly snake. Ben hid behind Emma, then Emma hid behind Ben. Then the dog hid behind Ben and Emma and said '*woof*'.

They scrambled away from the massive, scaly snake and saw a... lion! He was a friendly lion, but they did not know he was friendly. He showed them he was friendly.

They got a very, very long ride to the magical tree. The lion stopped at some vines.

They swung to the tree and got home.

Kitty McDiarmid (6)
Chagford CE Primary School, Newton Abbot

Untitled

... a magical pile of socks. 'This must be Sock Land,' said Ben.

'Yeah, it must be,' said Emma.

'Let's go on an adventure,' said Emma.

'Yes,' said Ben.

'Argh! That sock's alive and it's coming for us. Run for it!' said Ben.

'Argh!' said Emma. They ran for it.

Then a friendly sock saw how much trouble they were in, so he tried to help them.

He was called Super Sock. He could save the day. So he had an immense battle.

Super Sock distracted the bad sock, whilst Ben and Emma ran to the door in the tree.

Ember Hine (6)

Chagford CE Primary School, Newton Abbot

Charlotte's Magical Story

Ben and Emma saw a magic fairy castle with fairies flying around it. Emma went into the castle and saw the queen fairy.

One day, Emma saw a door and she found a key on the ground so she picked it up and opened the door. She saw a fairy.

The next day, Emma saw another magic door. She opened the door and saw a smelly troll.

The next day, Emma went to her friend's house and she saw a smelly house with a troll and a fairy. They had a party and they had a picnic. It was a nice party with balloons and streamers.

They went home with a present and they had streamers.

Charlotte Rose H (6)
Chagford CE Primary School, Newton Abbot

Poppy's Jungle Story

A jungle was through the magic door and they swung on some vines. Their dog even swung too. When they swung down, a snake suddenly appeared. Emma and Ben were very scared. They had to run and run because the snake was very fast.

Just then, a massive lion appeared and scared the snake away. Again, they were very scared.

Guess what? The lion gave the children a ride.

They swung on some vines again, then they saw the door again.

Poppy Lola Dooley-Cloke (6)

Chagford CE Primary School, Newton Abbot

Gryffin's Jungle Story

It took them to a wild, bumpy jungle with waving grass and swinging branches. They were worried. They walked along.

As they were walking along, they saw a snake. It was a python. They were scared and it chased after them.

It snapped at them. Then they were out of breath. They found a lion and they asked him if he could take them on his back. They climbed on.

They were at the magic door and then they were home. They were happy.

Gryffin Gordon Clark (6)
Chagford CE Primary School, Newton Abbot

Anastasia's Magical Story

They found an enchanted princess castle. A sparkly, beautiful enchanted castle.

It was a fairy's and she shimmered and sparkled in the sun.

Suddenly, a pig spoke to them and the dog barked. The fairy said, 'Don't worry, it's OK.'

The dog liked the candy and the dog was called Barbie. The dog licked and licked.

The fairy asked if they would like to go to her birthday party.

They got some presents.

Anastasia Elizabeth Leaman (6)

Chagford CE Primary School, Newton Abbot

Lily's Superhero Story

Once upon a time, there was a superhero called Poppy. She was the best superhero ever.
One day there was a burglar. Poppy said, 'What are you doing?' The burglar kept on running.
Then Ben and Poppy caught him and they called the police.
The police put him in jail and he never escaped again.
Ben and Poppy had saved the day.
Then they flew back to the magic door and teleported back home.

Lily Grace Sargent (6)
Chagford CE Primary School, Newton Abbot

Charlie's Superhero Story

Once upon a time there were two superheroes and a dog.

Whilst they were flying, they saw a burglar running happily.

They flew down and said, 'You're coming with us.' The robber was nervous.

Then the robber got sent to jail and he was upset.

They got rewarded and became the best superheroes.

Then they said, 'It's time we went.' They flew back to the door.

Charlie Mathewson-Coombe (6)
Chagford CE Primary School, Newton Abbot

Noah's Superhero Story

Two super-cool heroes glided with a scruffy, fluffy, super dog. They zoomed to save the day.
A robber stole money from the city. They saw the robber.
Next, they shot ahead of the robber. They said, 'What are you doing?'
They phoned the police. He was locked in prison.
They won a bag and the dog won one too.
They zoomed back to the tree.

Noah Tarbet (7)
Chagford CE Primary School, Newton Abbot

Dragon Land

In Dragon Land, they turned into bad and good dragons.

One of them was eating a scared mouse because he was hungry.

A robot came too and the dragon dog threw a bone because he couldn't control himself.

The king and queen dragons kissed and the good and bad dragons turned back and found the door in the tree.

They turned human again like magic.

Lewis Edward Henry Litwinski (6)
Chagford CE Primary School, Newton Abbot

Matthew's Superhero Story

Once upon a time there were two superheroes and a dog.
Suddenly, a robber came and he stole £1,000.
Emma and Ben saw him and then they swooped down gently and caught him.
Emma and Ben took the robber and flew with him to prison. The police were angry with the robber. Ben and Emma got ten medals and the dog got a bone.

Matthew Cooper (8)
Chagford CE Primary School, Newton Abbot

Junior's Superhero Story

... Superhero Land. They could fly higher than the moon.

Then they saw a bad guy.

'What are you doing? You are stealing treasure.'

They trapped the bad guy. He tried to get out but he couldn't.

The superheroes beat the bad guy.

Then they went to the door in the tree.

Junior Andrew Mackenzie (6)

Chagford CE Primary School, Newton Abbot

Harry's Superhero Story

... a land of witches and superheroes. They went to the bank and the robber came with them too.
He took all the shiny cash and money.
The superheroes stopped him and put him in jail.
He was sad.
Ben and Emma saved the day.

Harry Thynne (6)
Chagford CE Primary School, Newton Abbot

Karson's Jungle Story

Once upon a time there was a little boy called Ben and the little girl was called Emma. The children were walking down the street. The children were walking and then the children saw a magic door. The magic door took them to the jungle. The children swung on the ropes.

The children were tired so they saw a van. They knocked on the van. There was a window. The window opened. There was a man so they ran away.

The children ran away from a snake. He was scary. The children ran and ran and ran and they were tired. They went behind a tree so the snake couldn't get them.

The lion came out, the children were scared of the lion. So the lion took them on a ride.

They were not tired, they were laughing. So they went to the forest. The lion was laughing.

The little boy and girl went to the trees.They went to a park. They played and played until they saw another dog.

Karson Jay Densley (5)
Cheddar Grove Primary School, Bristol

Lucie's Magical Story

A magical castle was very far away from where Emma and Ben were standing. They were so surprised when they saw it. They kept walking towards it in amazement, with Boris their white poodle beside them.

As they were walking they approached a beautiful fairy sitting on a mushroom. Boris, poked his tongue out and went *woof!*

Along came an unsuspecting troll that said, 'Hello!'. Emma and Ben froze like a statue when they first saw him. They were very surprised.

The troll started talking to Emma and Ben, whilst the fairy listened to everything that was being said.

Ben, Emma and Boris followed the troll through a door, to a house that was made of candy. Boris loves candy and ran over to the house with his tongue out, drooling and tail wagging, ready to lick the candy. It had ginger tiles for the roof.

In the house was a party, Ben and Emma had a smile on their faces. They enjoyed the party and had a lot of cakes.

They took some cake home for their tea. Emma, Ben and Boris were dancing and singing all the way, through the magical door and back home again.

Lucie Phillips (6)
Cheddar Grove Primary School, Bristol

Lillie-May's Jungle Story

The magic door took Ben and Emma to the jungle. They swung on some vines. They were very long. They went further in the jungle.

They wanted to go home. The dog felt he heard a *hisss* sound. 'I think we're in a snake forest,' said Emma.

'Watch out for snakes!' said Ben. They met a snake. The snake was not friendly. They ran and ran until they were tired. Finally they got away from the snake. But it was very scary living in the jungle. Then they saw a lion. He was friendly. The lion let them go on his back.

'This is fun,' said Emma.

'And bumpy too,' said Ben.

The lion was very fast. The lion took them home.

'This is a secret,' said Emma, 'I made a map and saw the magic door.'

They finally got home and they lived happily ever after.

Lillie-May Allen (5)

Cheddar Grove Primary School, Bristol

Emily's Magical Story

Inside the magical palace was a queen who was waiting for her dinner. They walked inside and found a little garden.

The queen let them go in it. Then they both went, 'Eek!' because there was a little fairy that looked very sad. Emma said, 'What is the matter?'

The fairy said, 'I can't find my friend.' Suddenly a big, brown troll appeared and said, 'My name is Brunch.' He led them to a special house.

The house was made of cookies and they all went inside. The troll said it was his house. The dog found a candy cane and didn't let go of it.

Then the troll gave a gift to the fairy but the fairy didn't think she deserved it so she gave it to Emma and Ben.

They both went home and lived happily every after.

Emily Rose Newman (6)
Cheddar Grove Primary School, Bristol

Samuel's Magical Story

Emma and Ben walked to a magical land full of all different kinds of things. The first thing they saw was a castle, they were so excited.

Next they found a fairy on a mushroom. She felt sad. The dog tried doing amazing tricks but it was no use.

One fairy stole her powers but she got her powers back.

A little monster was their new best friend. He could make them go anywhere.

He made them go to a candy house. The dog munched the street light, it was five feet tall. They then went inside.

It was the next day and it was the monster's birthday. They gave him cake. The monster was nine years old.

At the end of the day they took their party bags and ate some cakes. So they took their dog back to their home town.

Samuel Medway (6)
Cheddar Grove Primary School, Bristol

Mason's Pirate Story

Ben and Emma were on a pirate island. Emma and Ben found a boat. They rowed across the stream. A while later they spotted something in the distance. It was a treasure island. They found gold and diamonds. Emma found a tiara. Their dog found a golden crown. It was a bit heavy.

After a while a pirate showed up. He said, 'Do you want to come on my pirate ship?'

Ben was nervous but he said, 'Yes.'

The pirate tricked them. He wanted them to walk the plank because they stole his treasure. He was very upset.

Luckily some dolphins saved Emma and Ben. They made friends. They played for a little while until they had to go home.

The dolphins took them to shore. They said bye and ran back.

Mason Chick (6)

Cheddar Grove Primary School, Bristol

Ella's Magical Story

There was a magical castle that was very far away from where they were standing. They were very surprised when they saw it.

The queen showed them a fairy in the garden and when they saw her they went, 'Eek!' in surprise and they said, 'Hello.'

Ben and Emma met a troll and said, 'Eek!' They ran away because the troll said, 'I'm going to eat you because I am hungry.'

The troll went back home and he said, 'Hello, shall we play together?'

They walked back to their house.

Ben and Emma went to a party and the dog and the troll were there. They all danced and they were happy.

Ben and Emma finished the party and they went back home. They said, goodbye.

Ella Grace Baxter (6)
Cheddar Grove Primary School, Bristol

Autumn's Magical Story

There was a fairy castle. When they went inside the castle they found a guard from the palace. He took them into the dungeon and they escaped and found a fairy. She was so small. The fairy asked them, 'Where have you come from?'

Emma and Ben replied, 'We have come from a magic door.'

Suddenly a troll appeared and the troll said, 'Hello, why are you here?'

'We do not know why we are here.'

So the troll took them to a gingerbread house and the dog looked at a candy cane and ate it. It was yummy. Then he ate the house!

They had a party and it was amazing. They got presents and hats, also cake. It was yummy. Then they left the party but it was fun.

Autumn Clothier (7)

Cheddar Grove Primary School, Bristol

Demi's Space Story

Emma and Ben came out to space. They couldn't believe what they were seeing and then they landed on an island.

The boy crashed into a star in the sky.

An alien saw the little boy. He went closer and they looked around. Soon they were friends!

Because the alien was so kind he went to take them to his house, and even the dog.

He said, 'This is real!' The alien said.

'Yes,' the boy said, 'there's a scary monster.'

'This is scary!'

The alien said, 'Let me say this is my brother.'

The boy said, 'We'll be going now Alien. See you soon.'

The girl soon kind of missed her new alien friend.

Demi Selway (6)

Cheddar Grove Primary School, Bristol

Jessica's Magical Story

One day Emma and Ben walked into a forest and then found a castle. Inside there was a fairy, it was talking to Emma and Ben.

She said, 'There might be some scary stuff in here. But don't worry because they aren't real!' So they walked into the castle.

They met a troll and the fairy was wrong. But the troll said, 'Hello,' and said, 'Can we have a party?' So they went in the troll's house. They even had a cake. They loved it, it looked yummy.

So they had a party and danced and sang and had some cake. They loved it. Then they said, goodbye. So they went home. They sneakily had some cake. When they got home they went to sleep.

Jessica Louise Simmons (7)

Cheddar Grove Primary School, Bristol

Molly's Jungle Story

Emma and Ben saw a vine and they climbed it. There was a monkey and the monkey said, 'You can come with me.'
Then they saw a snake but it wasn't a mean snake, it was a kind snake and it cuddled Emma and Ben. Then it said, 'You can go and see more animals now.'
Emma and Ben said, 'Thank you.'
Then they were suddenly running away from the snake because the snake was lying.
When they got away from the snake, they said, 'There's a lion.' But the lion was a kind lion because it let them have a ride on his back.
Then the lion went further and further. Then they got tired and they swung home to the tree and went home.

Molly Rogers (6)
Cheddar Grove Primary School, Bristol

Charlie's Magical Story

Emma and Ben were taken to a magical world with a castle. They were excited, they wanted to go inside but they wanted to go home.

There was a very small fairy that said, 'Hello, why are you here?'

'Because we didn't know anyone was in here.'

'Oh no, who are you?'

'I am the King of the world, I tell everyone what to do but I do some stuff too.'

Then a troll took them to a house. The troll said, 'Come in here, you will be safe in there, it is nice.'

There was a party in the house. There were presents, cake and party hats and party food.

They were going home and they were really happy.

Charlie Brice (6)

Cheddar Grove Primary School, Bristol

Brendon's Pirate Story

Suddenly Ben and Emma sat in a boat. They rowed the boat and they were scared. They found a spade, Ben picked it up.

They went to Pirate Land. They dug out a treasure chest. They were excited But Ben wasn't scared. It was too late. Then there was a pirate. He was bad, he wanted to bring Emma.

The pirate did bring Emma. Ben then walked the plank. Emma was scared and the dog was too.

The dolphins were in the sea. They smiled. The dolphins jumped out of the water. The dog was smiling.

They got to land and they ran to the magic door. They got to the door but the door was closed...

Brendon Kelly (6)
Cheddar Grove Primary School, Bristol

Alfie's Pirate Story

One sunny day Emma and Ben were on a wooden boat sailing in the sea and they had the dog on the boat and they were happy.

Then they found a box of money and they found some coconuts. They looked so happy they might take it away.

Then they met a captain who didn't have any treasure and wanted treasure and so much gold. The kids had to walk the plank for stealing treasure but they were so sorry. They still needed to walk the plank.

But the dolphins were kind. They caught them. The dolphins were happy and lovely.

The kids were happy. They went home for a snack to eat.

Alfie Barber (6)

Cheddar Grove Primary School, Bristol

Isabella's Jungle Story

In a jungle they swung on the monkey swings. They were swinging until they couldn't hold on anymore. Then they met a scary snake and they were scared of the scary snake. So scared that they ran away. Then they ran and ran until they couldn't run any faster. Then they cried and cried and then they stopped.
Then they met a lion and they were worried but he was a nice lion and even the dog was scared.
Then they knew that he was a nice lion and he took them all for a ride.
Then they found their home and they were really happy.

Isabella Muscat (6)
Cheddar Grove Primary School, Bristol

Alice's Pirate Story

On a desert island they travelled in a boat with their dog. They travelled and travelled until they got to a desert island.

They got out of the boat and found a treasure box. They put on a crown but he spotted a pirate boat. A pirate got out of the boat and said, 'Hey get your hands off my treasure and come with us.

They were told to walk the plank. A dolphin spotted them and rescued them.

They were having a good time then they had to get off.

Soon they arrived and they played and sang songs until they went back home.

Alice Gommo (6)

Cheddar Grove Primary School, Bristol

Oliver's Jungle Story

Emma and Ben were in a jungle. Suddenly their dog started to bark at a snake. So they got scared. They ran away.

The snake got tired so they stopped. They went deeper into the jungle. Then they heard a lion, he was near.

The lion said, 'Do you want a ride?'

They said, 'Yes.' So they got on the lion.

The lion said, 'I can take you anywhere.' So they said,'Thank you for the ride.'

They saw a door then got off the lion and went near the door. They walked through the door and went home.

Oliver West (5)
Cheddar Grove Primary School, Bristol

Lottie's Magical Story

The door took Ben and Emma to a magical land where it was sunny every day. Emma loved it there, so did Ben.

Soon a fairy appeared. She said, 'I have lost my tiara.'

Emma and Ben said, they would help. Then they had fairy wings.

The fairy took them to a troll's party and it was his birthday. Emma wanted to have a party.

Then they decorated the room and baked a cake for the party. It was about to start.

The party started and everybody loved the party.

When they left the troll gave them the tiara.

Lottie Cartwright (6)

Cheddar Grove Primary School, Bristol

Gracie's Jungle Story

A dog and Ben were swinging, then the dog disappeared somewhere. Ben and Emma went to look for him.
The boy saw a snake. The snake looked mad. The boy looked scared so did the girl.
The snake went to get them so they ran.
They saw a lion. He helped them. He ran as fast as he could. They got back on the lion then they found their dog.
It jumped over the plant. It ran as fast as it could. Then they got off. They said, 'Thanks!'
They got back on the vine. They found their dog. They went out the door.

Gracie-Lou Cornish (5)
Cheddar Grove Primary School, Bristol

Sonny's Pirate Story

One day Emma and Ben went to a treasure hunt and they were riding a boat. They found an island with lots of treasure.

The dog had a crown on his head and on the island there was a lovely pine tree.

After that they saw a real pirate come along and the dog was worried. The pirate had a sword.

They had to go on the ship. They had to walk the plank and they were really worried.

After that some dolphins saved them and they were very happy. The dolphins were friendly

They then walked home.

Sonny Alfie Kibby (6)

Cheddar Grove Primary School, Bristol

Lacey's Pirate Story

Emma and Ben were rowing a boat. When they were rowing the boat they went through a magic door.

They landed on a treasure island and they saw a treasure box. They opened it and they saw a pirate with a sword in his hand.

He made a punishment. He made Emma walk the plank. There were dolphins that came up and saved her life.

Emma and Ben liked the dolphins so they swam together. They then jumped off the dolphins and went to the tree.

They went through the door and lived happily ever after.

Lacey Gillett (5)
Cheddar Grove Primary School, Bristol

Leon's Space Story

Emma and Ben went to space and met an alien. The alien liked them. Then Emma and Ben went to catch stars. Then the alien and his friends kidnapped them because they thought Emma and Ben were stealing the stars. The alien took Emma and Ben to a place where they didn't know where they were. But then Emma and Ben said, sorry. So the aliens gave Emma and Ben a ride. But then a large alien tried to eat the spaceship but luckily they got away so the alien dropped Emma and Ben home.

Leon Green (6)
Cheddar Grove Primary School, Bristol

Alexa's Jungle Story

Once upon a time on a sunny day, Emma and Ben were walking the dog. Suddenly the dog started barking at the magic door hidden in the tree. And it took them to the jungle.

When they got there they met a cute lion and they rode on his back.

They jumped over a cliff. When they got back to the spot a lion the lion was worn out.

He came out of the jungle and the children disappeared at home and the lion went with them. They asked their mum if they could keep him.

Alexa Lowe Wilson-Rawlings (6)
Cheddar Grove Primary School, Bristol

Charlotte's Pirate Story

Once upon a time they got a boat on a cold river.
They got on an island to find some treasure.
They dug and dug until they found some treasure.
When a pirate came and said, 'You don't get my treasure. I am going to get you. I've now got you on my boat, you are going to walk the plank!'
Then some dolphins came to help them.
They got on them. 'Take us home,' they said.
They found the tree. They had an adventure.

Charlotte Hill (5)

Cheddar Grove Primary School, Bristol

Mariah's Jungle Story

In a jungle Emma and Ben swung on the long wavy, vines and even the dog. They were singing on the vines.

Then they fell off and a snake was alone. It wanted to be their friend but they weren't sure about that. They ran away and they almost fell over.

A lion came and they didn't like the lion either. They asked the lion to have a ride on the lion's back. The lion said, 'Yes.'

They swung back to the tree.

Mariah Curtis (6)
Cheddar Grove Primary School, Bristol

Holly's Jungle Story

Ben and Emma were walking the dog. Suddenly the dog was barking at a magic door. They hid in a tree. Emma and Ben opened the door. They went inside. They swung on vines. They swung down and saw a snake. They fought the snake. He was not friendly so they ran away.

They saw a lion. They went and the lion was friendly.

They went and rode on the lion.

They went and they swung on the vines. They opened the door and they went back home.

Holly Martin (5)

Cheddar Grove Primary School, Bristol

Harmony's Jungle Story

It was a jungle. The children climbed down the vines to get to the jungle floor.

The children were scared of the snake, they ran off.

They stopped for a minute. 'Run!' they said. 'Run away from the snake!'

One lion said hi to the children. He asked, 'Where are you going?'

'We are trying to get home.'

The lion gave them a ride back to the door.

They climbed up the vines to get home.

Harmony McGauley (5)
Cheddar Grove Primary School, Bristol

Millie's Pirate Story

Ben and Emma floated away. They looked at the sand.

They looked all around the desert. They found treasure and played with it.

A pirate popped out. He said, 'Ha, ha, ha, give me the treasure.'

The pirate let Ben walk the plank. Emma had shaky legs. The dog was grumpy.

Some dolphins came and took them to land.

Emma, Ben and the dog went on a walk.

They went back through the door and they looked like pirates.

Millie Brookman (5)

Cheddar Grove Primary School, Bristol

Harry's Jungle Story

Emma and Ben went on a trip. They went on the ropes. The dog found a door.

They went through the door.

They saw a snake, they were scared.

They ran away because they were scared of the snake.

They saw a lion, 'I think you would like a lift back.'

They said, 'OK!'

They went on his back and had a good journey back.

They went to the door. They went through and they went home.

Harry Scott Gribble (6)

Cheddar Grove Primary School, Bristol

Miley's Magical Story

One sunny day Emma and Ben were walking the dog. Then they saw a castle and they were laughing about the castle.

They went in the castle and they saw a fairy. Emma and Ben were scared. They saw a troll and the troll was scary and Emma and Ben were scared too.

The troll took them to a gingerbread house. Then they were happy again.

They had a party with the troll.

Then they went home to their warm house.

Miley Rose Gazzard (6)
Cheddar Grove Primary School, Bristol

Davi's Superhero Story

'Look a robber is on the loose, let's get him!' the boy said.

They landed. The robber laughed and laughed. He said, 'No one can stop me now!'

'We will get you,' they said.

'No you won't, I have money,' he said.

They both caught him and threw him in prison. Everybody yelled, 'Hooray!'

They then went to the magic door and flew back home.

Davi Egho (6)
Cheddar Grove Primary School, Bristol

Finley's Jungle Story

In the jungle Ben and Emma swung on vines.
Suddenly they saw a snake.
The snake was very friendly, he showed them the way.
They then escaped and ran away.
They came to a lion who showed them the way. He asked if they wanted to ride on his back?
They said, 'Yes please.'
The lion took them to the door and they said, 'Thank you.'
They were soon back home.

Finley Forristal (6)
Cheddar Grove Primary School, Bristol

Alfie's Magical Story

In a magical place they saw a castle. They were outside, the dog was so happy.

They went inside the castle. They saw a fairy, it was sitting on a mushroom with grass on the ground.

A man was looking stinky and smelly and he waved at them.

The smelly man showed them his candy house

It was the smelly man's birthday. Emma and Ben had birthday hats.

They then went back.

Alfie Hazell (6)
Cheddar Grove Primary School, Bristol

Archie's Pirate Story

Ben and Emma were walking the dog but the dog started barking.

They saw a magic door and they opened the door and went through.

The magic door took Ben and Emma to the pirates and the pirates were bad.

One pirate said, 'Get off my chest!'

The pirate made them walk the plank.

Some dolphins took the children.

They lived happily ever after.

Archie Isom (5)

Cheddar Grove Primary School, Bristol

Harrison's Jungle Story

The children went into a jungle and swung on a
vine and fell down.
They met a snake and the snake hissed and Ben
said, 'Why is there a snake?'
Ben and Emma ran away and then Ben got a wand
and killed the snake.
And met a lion and made friends with the lion.
Then Ben and Emma got on Lion and Ben said,
'Come on!' and they went home.

Harrison Edward Govier (6)
Cheddar Grove Primary School, Bristol

Frankie's Jungle Story

Once upon a time Ben and Emma went to the jungle.

Next they fell off the vines. Next they came to a snake.

They ran away from the snake, they ran quickly.

They saw the lion, it was friendly. The boy poked his tail.

Then the lion jumped then the lion gave them a lift. It was good.

They went through the door and they were back in the park.

Frankie Baker (5)

Cheddar Grove Primary School, Bristol

Ruby's Pirate Story

The boat started to move, Emma and Ben were scared.
It took them to an island. They saw a naughty pirate. He stole the treasure.
He made them walk the plank. The dog was scared. Emma was scared.
The boy went to a dolphin. He was frightened.
They fell on the dolphins, they were friendly.
They went back. The dog was a pirate. Ben was too.

Ruby Jones (5)
Cheddar Grove Primary School, Bristol

Lucy's Jungle Story

Ben and Emma were in a jungle. They swung on vines. Emma and Ben were falling down, then there was a snake.
Ben and Emma and the dog ran from the snake. The snake was trying to find them.
The snake was chasing them.
They met a lion. He was friendly.
They rode on the lion's back. He was a bad lion.
They soon got home.

Lucy-Lei Katrina Campho (6)
Cheddar Grove Primary School, Bristol

Ellis' Jungle Story

One sunny day Emma and Ben were walking the dog. Suddenly the dog started to bark at a magic door hidden in a tree.

They were in the jungle. They met a snake and they were friends.

The snake chased them because they were playing tag.

They met a lion and rode it.

It was fun.

They went through the door again and back home.

Ellis Pitman (7)

Cheddar Grove Primary School, Bristol

Justin's Superhero Story

Emma and Ben turned into superheroes and flew around and saw a robber.

The robber had just escaped from jail and robbed a bank.

Emma and Ben caught him and he went back to jail.

He said, 'I will get you superheroes!'

Emma and Ben got a medal from the guys from the jail.

Emma and Ben found the door and went home.

Justin Cove (6)

Cheddar Grove Primary School, Bristol

Dylan's Superhero Story

They were superheroes and the dog was one too.
They were on patrol and they saw a thief and they
flew down.
Then they went down and caught the thief. They
put him in jail and he was very sad. Then the thief
gave up, so well done!
But it was not over yet because they had to be
awarded. Then they were going to go home.

Dylan Noel (6)
Cheddar Grove Primary School, Bristol

Zack's Pirate Story

One sunny day Emma and Ben were walking the
dog. Suddenly it started barking at the door
hidden in a tree.
They opened the door...
The pirate wanted them to walk the plank.
Emma and Ben were scared. Ben walked the plank.
The friendly dolphins got Ben and Emma.
Ben found the door and they ran to the door.

Zackary Daniel Brice (5)
Cheddar Grove Primary School, Bristol

Naomi's Jungle Story

Emma and Ben swung on vines, until they saw a snake.
They were scared but the snake was friendly.
Ben and Emma saw a lion.
'Hop on my back,' said the lion. They hopped on, it was bumpy.
Ben and Emma were sitting on the lion's back.
Ben and Emma got to the door and it took them home.

Naomi Allen (5)
Cheddar Grove Primary School, Bristol

Lennon's Space Story

Emma and Ben travelled to space and landed. They caught the stars and they saw a big alien. The alien was nice. The alien played with Emma and Ben.

The alien helped them. They picked the pretty stars.

The alien flew and lifted them up.

The alien was friendly. They got in and he took them home.

Lennon Ross Govier (6)

Cheddar Grove Primary School, Bristol

Freya's Jungle Story

Suddenly Ben and Emma saw a jungle. Then they saw some vines.

They saw a snake in the jungle. The boy was scared. The snake chased them. They ran away.

They saw a lion and the lion was friendly.

The children sat on the lion and the lion ran.

They got home into their tree house.

Freya Jones (5)
Cheddar Grove Primary School, Bristol

Jessica's Magical Story

One sunny day Emma and Ben were walking the dog. There was a castle and they opened the door and found lots of magic.

They walked into the castle and found a little fairy on a toadstool.

They saw a troll and they were scared.

But soon they became best friends and had a party.

Jessica Evans (6)

Cheddar Grove Primary School, Bristol

Charlie's Pirate Story

One day Emma and Ben were in a boat with the dog.
Ben saw a pirate ship. Ben was frightened and they wanted to hide.
They went to the pirate ship. He wanted the treasure.
Ben went on the plank.
Some dolphins came and took them to the door.
They were back home.

Caroline Mark Hazell (5)
Cheddar Grove Primary School, Bristol

Beau's Jungle Story

A dog and a boy and girl swung on vines. They were happy.

They were frightened of the snake. The snake got angry.

The snake ran after them.

They ran into a lion. The lion was hunting.

The lion said, 'Do you want a ride?'

Off they went home.

Beau Hickery (5)

Cheddar Grove Primary School, Bristol

Brooke's Pirate Story

Emma and Ben rowed on the boat.

Emma found treasure. Ben was afraid. He saw a pirate ship.

The pirate said, 'That is my treasure!'

The pirate made them walk the plank. 'Help!' they said.

The dolphin set them free.

They ran home.

Brooke Turner (5)
Cheddar Grove Primary School, Bristol

Lily's Jungle Story

Once Ben and Gemma were climbing the vines through the jungle.

They flew down onto the floor.

Then a snake was chasing them.

The dog barked and barked. Suddenly a lion came.

The lion gave Emma, Ben and the dog a lift.

Then they went home.

Lily Avril Callen (6)

Cheddar Grove Primary School, Bristol

Liam's Jungle Story

One sunny day Emma and Ben were walking the dog.
Suddenly the dog started barking at a magic door hidden in a tree.
They opened the door...
Emma ran and Ben ran from the snake. Then a kind lion came to take them home. So the lion took them home.

Liam Dunn (5)
Cheddar Grove Primary School, Bristol

Jude's Pirate Story

It took them to a door, Emma and Ben opened the door and they found a boat.
Ben saw a galloping ship. Emma was happy, the dog was too.
They were worried
Ben walked the plank.
They rode some dolphins
They ran through the trees.

Jude Clark (5)
Cheddar Grove Primary School, Bristol

Shay's Superhero Story

Ben and Emma were walking to the door. Then they turned into superheroes and they caught a robber.

The robber was so slow and they were good superheroes.

The robber was sad he was in jail.

He was a bad guy.

The superheroes were happy.

Shay Goff (7)

Cheddar Grove Primary School, Bristol

Ria's Pirate Story

Ben and Emma were at the pirate world. Emma
and Ben rowed the boat to find the pirate treasure
They found money, gold and tiaras.
A pirate found them.
They walked the plank.
They rode on two dolphins
They ran to the door.

Ria Ashley Williamson (5)

Cheddar Grove Primary School, Bristol

Willow's Jungle Story

One sunny day Emma and Ben were walking and saw a door.
They opened the door and saw a snake.
They ran away from the snake.
They met a friendly lion.
The lion gave them a ride.
They went back through the door.

Willow Young (5)
Cheddar Grove Primary School, Bristol

Lily's Pirate Story

Ben was rowing, the sun was shining.
They were soon digging for treasure and the girl
was wearing a crown.
The pirate came to see them.
There was a ship.
They rode a dolphin, it was fun.
They saw a tree house.

Lily May (5)
Cheddar Grove Primary School, Bristol

Tahlia's Pirate Story

One sunny day Emma and Ben were walking the
dog. Suddenly the dog started barking.
Emma looked pretty.
The pirate got cross.
The children had to walk the plank.
The dolphins saved them.
The children ran back.

Tahlia Zylinska (5)
Cheddar Grove Primary School, Bristol

Albert's Jungle Story

In the jungle Ben and Emma swung on some vines. Suddenly they fell.

They saw a snake. They ran into the middle of the jungle.

They saw a lion. They were scared.

They rode the lion.

They noticed they were home.

Albert Delahunty (6)
Cheddar Grove Primary School, Bristol

Dylan's Superhero Story

Ben and Emma went into space. They fell to Earth
and then they saw a robber.

They saw the robber and he had some money.

The robber stopped.

They put the robber in jail.

They got badges.

They flew home.

Dylan Colgan (6)

Cheddar Grove Primary School, Bristol

Megan's Pirate Story

Ben and Emma went to a boat and found treasure.
Ben saw a pirate ship.
He saw the treasure chest.
The pirate made Ben walk the plank.
Two dolphins came and they jumped.
Ben and Emma then got home.

Megan Allen (5)

Cheddar Grove Primary School, Bristol

Ava's Jungle Story

Emma and Ben swung through the door.
They saw a snake in the tree. The children were
petrified.
The children ran for it.
They saw a lion.
The lion took the children to a door.
And they were home.

Ava Carnevale (5)
Cheddar Grove Primary School, Bristol

Callum's Jungle Story

Emma and Ben were swinging on the vines.
They met a snake who was lonely.
The snake tried and tried to control them.
They met a scary lion.
They had a ride on him.
They went to their house.

Callum Colgan (6)

Cheddar Grove Primary School, Bristol

Woody's Jungle Story

Emma and Ben climbed on trees.
They met a snake. They were frightened.
They ran away. 'Oh no!'
They met a lion that was friendly.
He gave them a lift
They swung home.

Woody Milkins (6)
Cheddar Grove Primary School, Bristol

Harley's Pirate Story

Emma and Ben went to a boat.
Emma found the treasure.
The pirate was angry.
The children walked the plank.
The dolphins saved them.
They ran to the door.

Harley Court (5)

Cheddar Grove Primary School, Bristol

Tayah's Magical Story

Ben and Emma found a magical land, 'Wow!'
'Woof, woof, woof, woof.'
Suddenly there was a fairy flying by the dog.
Suddenly here was a lovely lion.
They found a candy house. The dog had a piece of candy.
They had cake. They had a party. They all had presents.
They went home with a party hat on.

Tayah Lawrence-Decker (5)
King's Park Academy, Bournemouth

Alicja's Magical Story

Ben and Emma saw a castle.
Suddenly, Ben and Emma saw a girl with wings.
Then Ben and Emma saw a monster.
The monster showed Ben and Emma a chocolate house.
The monster showed Ben and Emma a super party.
Ben and Emma went back home.

Alicja Damasiewicz (5)
King's Park Academy, Bournemouth

Marcie's Magical Story

Ben and Emma suddenly saw a castle.
Ben and Emma suddenly saw a toadstool with a fairy.
They saw a lion, the lion was friendly.
They went to go in the lovely house.
They had a party at his house.
They went in the magic door.

Marcie Goodchild (6)
King's Park Academy, Bournemouth

Sebastian's Jungle Story

Ben and Emma were in the jungle and they were swinging.

Suddenly they saw a snake.

The snake was going to make them dizzy but they ran.

They saw a lion it was a nice lion.

They had a ride on the lion.

They went back home.

Sebastian Andrei Bran (5)

King's Park Academy, Bournemouth

Ethan's Space Story

Ben and Emma are in space.
Suddenly they see an alien.
Then the alien's spaceship sucks them up.
Ben and Emma are having fun.
Suddenly a monster alien is near.
The alien drops them off at the magic door.

Ethan Frampton (5)
King's Park Academy, Bournemouth

João's Superhero Story

Ben and Emma were flying in the sky.
Suddenly a burglar appeared.
Ben and Emma ran after the burglar.
Ben and Emma arrested it.
Ben and Emma got a badge on their chests.
Ben and Emma got the other tree.

João Serrao (5)
King's Park Academy, Bournemouth

Daisy's Pirate Story

Ben and Emma suddenly saw their boat sailing.
They found treasure.
A pirate took their treasure.
The pirate made Ben walk the plank.
Both the dolphins came to get them.
The dolphins took them home.

Daisy Smee (5)
King's Park Academy, Bournemouth

Kelly's Magical Story

Ben and Emma went to a magical castle.
Ben and Emma found a fairy sat on a mushroom.
Then they saw a monkey.
They made their way to a sweet house.
They had a party.
They went home.

Kelly De Sousa (5)

King's Park Academy, Bournemouth

Patryk's Superhero Story

The superheroes were Ben and Emma.
They saw a burglar.
Suddenly they stopped the burglar.
They put the burglar under arrest.
They then walked to the door.
They flew to the house.

Patryk Mitera (5)
King's Park Academy, Bournemouth

Oliver's Superhero Story

Ben and Emma went to save the city as
superheroes.
Suddenly a burglar robbed the bank.
They caught the burglar.
He went to the prison.
They had a good time.
They went home.

Oliver Fay (5)
King's Park Academy, Bournemouth

Zuzanna's Superhero Story

Ben and Emma were superheroes.
Suddenly they saw a burglar.
Then they got the burglar.
They put the burglar in the jail.
Then they were happy.
They flew to the magic door.

Zuzanna Jakubowska (6)
King's Park Academy, Bournemouth

Samuel's Superhero Story

Ben and Emma were flying around town.
Suddenly the burglar ran from the superheroes.
Suddenly they caught him.
They put him in jail.
They got a badge.
They flew home.

Samuel Lee Edensor (5)

King's Park Academy, Bournemouth

Nicole's Magical Story

Ben and Emma found a castle.
Suddenly a fairy was there.
They found a lion.
They went to the fairy's house.
They had a happy birthday.
They were home.

Nicole Lipka (5)
King's Park Academy, Bournemouth

Alexander's Jungle Story

Ben and Emma went on ropes.

They saw a snake.

They ran away.

They saw a lion.

They rode on the lion.

They went home.

Alexander Wilson (5)

King's Park Academy, Bournemouth

Grace's Jungle Story

The jungle where they swing on long green vines.
They met a long snake with big red eyes.
The snake tried to eat the dog.
'Oh no, help us,' they said.
They then ran into a friendly lion.
The lion took them for a ride on his back.
They swung back on the green vines through the door and home again.

Grace Poole (7)
Trinity CE (VA) First School, Verwood

The Storyboards

Here are the fun storyboards children could choose from...

Jungle

Magical

Pirate

Space

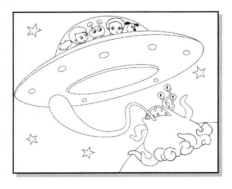

Superhero

First published in Great Britain in 2017 by:

Coltsfoot Drive
Peterborough
PE2 9BF
Telephone: 01733 890066
Website: www.youngwriters.co.uk

All Rights Reserved
Book Design by Spencer Hart
© Copyright Contributors 2017
SB ISBN 978-1-78624-972-2
Printed and bound in the UK by BookPrintingUK
Website: www.bookprintinguk.com
YB0306AZ

Young Writers Information

We hope you have enjoyed reading this book and that you will continue to in the coming years.

If you're a young writer who enjoys reading and creative writing, or the parent of an enthusiastic poet or story writer, do visit our website **www.youngwriters.co.uk**. Here you will find free competitions, workshops and games, as well as recommended reads, a poetry glossary and our blog.

If you would like to order further copies of this book, or any of our other titles give us a call or visit **www.youngwriters.co.uk**.

Young Writers
Remus House
Coltsfoot Drive
Peterborough
PE2 9BF

(01733) 890066
info@youngwriters.co.uk